A FUZZY-WUZZY SURPRISE!

When Carol pulled up in front of the ice rink, everyone thanked her for taking them on the trip to the animal shelter. Then Randi raced after Anna into Mr. Mullen's pro shop.

"My dad can drive you home as soon as he closes the shop," Anna offered.

"Okay," Randi said. "I guess I'll do some homework till then."

She sat down on the floor next to a stack of skate boxes. She reached into her backpack for her math book. But instead of feeling something smooth and cold, she felt something soft. And fuzzy.

And breathing!

Randi opened her bag wide. There, inside, sat *Socks*—the kitten she'd seen at the animal shelter!

Don't miss any of the fun titles in the Silver Blades

FIGURE EIGHTS series!

Randi's Pet Surprise

Effin Older

Illustrated by Marcy Ramsey

Created by Parachute Press, Inc.

A SKYLARK BOOK

NEW YORK · TORONTO · LONDON · SYDNEY · AUCKLAND

RL 2.6, 006–009

RANDI'S PET SURPRISE

A Skylark Book / November 1997

Skylark Books is a registered trademark of Bantam Books, a division of Bantam Doubleday Dell Publishing Group, Inc. Registered in U.S. Patent and Trademark Office and elsewhere.

Silver Blades® is a registered trademark of Parachute Press, Inc.

For information address: Bantam Doubleday Dell Books for Young Readers.

ISBN 0-553-48514-8

Published simultaneously in the United States and Canada

Bantam Books are published by Bantam Books, a division of Bantam Doubleday Dell Publishing Group, Inc. Its trademark, consisting of the words "Bantam Books" and the portrayal of a rooster, is Registered in U.S. Patent and Trademark Office and in other countries. Marca Registrada. Bantam Books, 1540 Broadway, New York, New York 10036.

PRINTED IN THE UNITED STATES OF AMERICA

OPM   0 9 8 7 6 5 4 3 2 1

*This book is for
Jim and Helen Hayford,
teachers extraordinaire.*

1

Hot Shots and Speed Demons!

"**H**urry up!" Woody Bowen called to Randi and Anna. "You're late for practice!"

Eight-year-old Randi Wong skidded to a stop next to Woody on the ice. She hated missing even the *tiniest* part of Friday-afternoon practice.

Woody tugged on her long dark braid and smiled. A second later Randi's best friend, Anna Mullen, slid up next to her.

Randi glanced around, catching her breath. Everyone in her skating group, Figure Eights, was gathered around their coach, Carol Crandall.

Max Harper pushed his glasses up on his nose. He pressed a button on his watch. "You're exactly two minutes and ten seconds late, Anna," he reported.

"Sorry, everybody," Anna apologized.

"We didn't miss anything important, did we?" Randi asked Carol.

Carol smiled and shook her head. "No, not yet."

Whew! Randi thought.

The members of Figure Eights skated together on Tuesday and Friday afternoons. It was the best part of Randi's week!

"The Figure Eights are having a skate-a-thon," Carol announced.

"A skate-a-thon?" Randi repeated. "What is that? *When* is it?"

"Hold on a minute and I'll tell you," Carol answered.

Randi had a hard time holding on a minute. She had a hard time even holding on a *second*!

"All the Figure Eights will skate in the skate-a-thon to raise money for the Best Buddies Animal Shelter. The shelter helps animals that don't have homes or owners who love them."

"Huh?" Randi frowned, confused. "How can *skating* raise money for homeless animals?"

"Especially when you're a klutzy skater like me," Samantha Rivers moaned.

"Or me," Kate Alvaro added.

"I know how skate-a-thons work," Woody said. "Everyone skates in a big circle. Over and over and over." He frowned. "Seems pretty dumb to me."

"Me too," Josh Freeman agreed.

Carol pulled Woody's baseball cap low over his wild red hair. "Hold on! There's more than that. For *this* skate-a-thon, you skate a different stroke for each circle around the rink."

"What kind of strokes?" Anna asked.

"Well, first you glide forward. Then you glide backward. Next you bunny-hop, scull forward, and scull backward. Then, if you're not too tired, you start all over again."

"Hey!" Randi exclaimed. "That doesn't sound stupid. It sounds totally fun! But I still don't understand how it will help the animals."

"I'm dividing the Figure Eights into two

teams," Carol explained. "Each team will ask people to *sponsor* it—that means they'll donate twenty-five cents for every lap the team completes around the rink. The team that raises the most money wins the skate-a-thon!"

"I'm going to get a jillion sponsors," Woody bragged. "How many days do I have till the skate-a-thon?"

"You'll all have to get your sponsors by next Saturday. That's only eight days away," Carol told them. "Can you do it?"

"Yeah!" all the Figure Eights cheered.

"Wow! This is the coolest!" Randi cried. "I love animals, and I *love* skating! Come on, Anna, let's practice!" She grabbed her best friend's hand.

"Wait, Randi!" Carol called. "We have to pick teams first."

"Oops! I got so excited, I forgot!" Randi said.

"Each team will have a captain," Carol explained. "And the captains will have a big job. They'll call special practice sessions, figure out how many sponsors their team has, and keep everyone excited about the skate-a-thon. But all

that hard work will be worth it for the captain who leads his or her team to victory!"

Cool! Randi thought. *I want to lead my team to victory!*

"Form a circle around me," Carol instructed. "I'll put on this blindfold and spin. When I stop, I'll point to someone. That person will be the captain of the first team, the Speed Demons."

Quickly the Figure Eights circled their coach. Carol spun around and around. Randi held her breath. *Please point to me,* she begged silently. *I want to be a captain.*

Carol stopped. She pointed—to Woody.

"Rats," Randi muttered under her breath.

"Yes!" Woody yelled. "Call me Captain Speed Demon!"

"Now, Woody," Carol said, "you get in the middle so *you* can pick the captain of the Hot Shots."

Woody moved to the middle of the circle. He put on the blindfold, and Carol gently spun him.

"Whooa!" Woody moaned as he spun around. He stopped. And he pointed—to Randi!

2

The Challenge

"All right! You're captain of the Hot Shots, Randi!" Woody yelled.

"Yay!" Randi shouted, hopping up and down.

"Now, each of you pick three people for your team," Carol instructed.

Randi quickly chose Anna, Max, and Kate.

Woody picked Josh, Samantha, and Frederika.

"Come on, Hot Shots!" Randi called to her team. "We'll have our first meeting right now. Follow me!" Randi led Anna, Max, and Kate to the far end of the rink.

"We'll meet on Monday and Wednesday after school for extra practice," she told her team. "And hey! We're off on Thursday because of that teachers' meeting! We can practice on Thursday morning too! Plus I'll check on your sponsor lists every day."

Randi looked at each member of her team. "We have to beat the Speed Demons!" she shouted. "Let's hear it, Hot Shots! What do we have to do?"

"Beat the Speed Demons!" Anna, Max, and Kate cheered.

"Now let's practice!" Randi cried.

With Randi leading them, the Hot Shots circled the rink. First, they glided forward.

That part is easy, Randi thought. "Okay, guys," she called. "Let's try going backward!" The Hot Shots started gliding backward.

"Whoa!" Randi heard someone behind her shout. She turned and saw Kate sprawled on the ice.

Randi rushed over to her friend. "Are you okay?" she asked.

"I'm fine," Kate said, brushing ice off her tights. "Sorry. I guess I'm not used to skating backward for that long."

The Hot Shots continued to circle the rink. But

a few minutes later, Max's skate blade caught a rough spot on the ice. He fell onto his knees. "Wow," he said. "Skating like this isn't easy."

"Keep trying," Randi encouraged her team. She led the Hot Shots in a lap of bunny-hops. "One-two-*hop*! One-two-*hop*!" she yelled.

Everyone hopped together.

While the Hot Shots were hopping, Randi stole a glance at the Speed Demons. Woody was leading them around the rink. And they were skating really well! Not even one of the Speed Demons had fallen down yet!

"Okay, let's try backward sculling," Randi called to her team.

She bent her knees, turned her toes in, and pushed her blades against the ice. Anna, Max, and Kate did the same. *Slowly* the Hot Shots sculled backward across the rink.

"Whoa! This is hard," Kate whined. "My legs are killing me!"

Once again Randi glanced over at the Speed Demons. They were sculling backward around the rink too. But they were moving twice as fast as the Hot Shots!

"Wow, Randi," Anna said softly. "The Speed Demons are skating really well. How are we ever going to beat them?"

"Don't worry," Randi told Anna. "We're going to work really hard on our skating. By the skate-a-thon, we'll be just as good as the Speed Demons."

"Do you think so?" Max asked.

"Absolutely," Randi promised.

Carol blew her whistle to end practice. "Good job, everybody," she said. "I have one more announcement. As a special treat, I've arranged for us to take a trip to the Best Buddies Animal Shelter on Monday afternoon. So remember to be here. And make sure you get permission from your parents."

"All right!" "Yeah!" the Figure Eights shouted.

"And remember—start getting your sponsors for our skate-a-thon next week!" Carol called as everyone made their way to the exit.

The Figure Eights crowded around the door. Randi smiled as she thought of visiting all the animals in the shelter.

She turned with a start when she felt someone poke her in the back. It was Woody. He smiled.

"Hey, Woody," Randi said. "Your team looks great on the ice."

"They sure do," Woody said. "And we're going to get a whole bunch of sponsors, too. There's no way your team is ever going to beat mine in the skate-a-thon, Randi. Not in a million years!"

"Oh yeah?" Randi answered. "Well, *I'm* going to get more sponsors than your whole team. And my team is going to win big-time. Just wait and see!"

3

No Pets Allowed

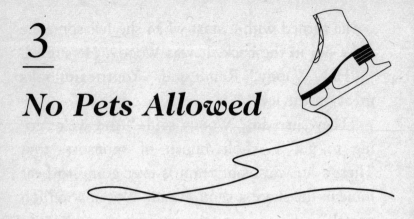

"Of course you can visit the animal shelter, Randi," Mrs. Wong said that night at dinner. "Having a skate-a-thon to help the animals sounds like a great idea."

Randi twisted a long piece of spaghetti around her fork. "I think it's cool," she agreed. She glanced around the table at her parents, her three brothers, and two of her three sisters. "And the Hot Shots are *definitely* going to win!"

"I'm glad you're so excited, Randi." Mr. Wong smiled. "But don't forget, winning isn't the most important thing. Helping the animals in the shelter is."

"I know," Randi replied.

"Being captain of your team sounds like a big job," Mrs. Wong said. "I hope it doesn't take time away from your homework and your skate practice and your chores around the house."

"Don't worry, Mom. I can handle everything. I promise." Randi felt a little shiver of excitement. "I can't wait to visit the shelter and see all the cute puppies and kittens and—"

"Puppies and kittens aren't as cool as my spider," twelve-year-old Henry said, interrupting Randi. "They're for *babies*, Randi." He stopped. "Hey! That must be what you are! Baby Randi! Baby Randi!" Henry repeated over and over.

"I am not a baby!" Randi bunched up her napkin and threw it across the table at Henry. She was sure he spent all his spare time thinking up new ways to torture her.

"My friend Megan got her puppy at an animal shelter. It's *soooo* adorable," ten-year-old Kristi put in.

"Puppies *are* cute!" Randi agreed. "Wouldn't it

be great to have a puppy right here in our house?"

Mrs. Wong frowned. "Randi, our family is way too busy to take care of a pet."

"But Kristi's got six goldfish," Randi pointed out. "And what about Henry's spider?"

"A spider doesn't need constant care," Mr. Wong explained. "Puppies and kittens do. I'm sorry, but it's too much for an eight-year-old to handle."

Randi sighed. She knew her parents were probably right.

"Well, now that that's settled, I think we should talk about Kristi's birthday!" Mrs. Wong suggested. "It's this Wednesday!"

"Can we get pizza for my birthday dinner?" Kristi asked.

Mrs. Wong laughed. "Actually, your father and I thought we'd take the whole family to Vinny's Pizzeria and then to a movie."

Kristi gave her mom a huge smile. "Cool!"

"Yay!" the six-year-old twins, Michael and Mark, shouted.

"The whole family can go. Even little Laurie,"

Mr. Wong said. He turned to wipe three-year-old Laurie's mouth.

Randi loved going for pizza with her family. But she was sorry that her fourteen-year-old sister, Jill, wouldn't be able to come too. Jill was away at skating school in Colorado.

Randi thought Jill was an awesome skater. She was going to the Olympics! And someday Randi wanted to be just like her.

After dinner Randi helped her dad with the dishes. As she wiped the clean dishes dry, she thought about the skate-a-thon.

I told everyone I'd get the most sponsors. I'd better start getting some right away! she said to herself.

She handed the last dry dish to her father. Then she darted into the living room.

"Mom," Randi asked, "will you take me out to get sponsors for the skate-a-thon?"

"Not right now, honey," Mrs. Wong answered. "I left some important papers at the office. Your dad's driving me there to get them. Would you and Kristi keep an eye on Laurie and the twins while I'm gone?"

Mrs. Wong's job at the travel agency kept her very busy. So Randi tried to help her mom any way she could.

"Uh—sure, Mom," Randi said, feeling a little disappointed.

"Thanks. We won't be long." Mrs. Wong hurried out the door.

Randi shrugged. *Oh, well, it's only the first night. There are eight days before the skate-a-thon. No one will be getting sponsors on the first night. Not even Woody!*

"Baby Ran-di!" Henry sang out from the kitchen doorway. "Telephone!"

"I am *not* a baby!" Randi yelled at Henry. Then she walked into the kitchen and picked up the phone. "Hello?"

"Hi, Randi. It's Anna. Guess what?"

"What?" Randi asked.

"I have ten sponsors already!"

"Wow!" Randi exclaimed. "How did you get so many?"

Anna chuckled. "I asked every customer who came into Dad's shop to sponsor me. And they all did!"

Anna's father, Mr. Mullen, owned the pro shop at the rink. He sold skates and skating outfits and lots of other cool stuff. Anna went there every day after school to help out.

"That's so awesome!" Randi cried.

"There was a hockey game at the rink tonight. I saw Woody asking the people there to sponsor him. I think he got a lot of names too." Anna paused. "So, how many sponsors do *you* have, Randi?"

"Uh . . . none yet. But I'm going to get tons," Randi answered.

"Better hurry up before *I* snag them all," Anna joked. "Or, even worse, before *Woody* does! Got to go. Bye!"

Randi hung up the phone. *Yikes!* she thought. *Anna and Woody already have lots of sponsors. If I'm going to be a good captain I'd better get some sponsors too. And soon!*

4

Surprise!

Three days later, at the Hot Shots' special Monday-afternoon practice, Randi had a hard time concentrating. She just couldn't wait to go to the animal shelter later that afternoon!

But she made sure to cheer on the Hot Shots as they skated.

"Okay," she called. "That's enough skating practice. Now I want to check on all your sponsors! I hope you found a bunch!"

"I know exactly how many I have," Max declared. "Five."

"I have six," Kate said proudly.

"I beat both of you," Anna announced. She

pushed a long brown curl off her cheek. "I have twelve!"

Wow! Randi thought. *I didn't know everyone had so many!*

Kate clapped her hands. "Excellent!" She turned to Randi. "How many sponsors did you get, Captain Randi?"

Randi felt her cheeks grow warm. "Well . . . ," she began, feeling embarrassed. "The truth is, I only have Mom and Dad. Oh, and Jill too. I asked her on the phone last night."

"Three!" Max exclaimed. "You're *captain,* and you only have *three* sponsors?"

"You said you'd have more than anybody!" Anna reminded her.

"Yeah, Randi, what are you waiting for?" Kate asked.

"Wait a minute. It's not my fault," Randi said. "On Friday night Kristi and I had to watch Laurie and the twins. Saturday Mom and Dad took everyone shopping for clothes. It took *all day!* Then Sunday we went to stupid Henry's soccer game and to visit my aunt and uncle. I had absolutely *no time!*"

19

Randi glanced at her teammates. Everyone frowned at her. "Look, guys," she said. "I promised I'd get the most sponsors—and that I'd be the best captain. I'm going to keep my promise."

"Well, you'd better get going if you want to be a better captain than Woody," Max said. "Today in school I heard him tell Josh he has *twenty* sponsors."

Randi paused. *Wow.* Woody had a lot of sponsors. She definitely needed to get more than that if her team was going to win!

"If Woody got twenty, I'll get twenty-five!" she said.

Anna looked amazed. "Whoa! Twenty-five? Do you really think you can get that many?"

Randi nodded. "No problem. I won't let the Hot Shots down!"

"Hey, guys!" Randi turned and saw Carol waving from the bleachers. "It's time to go to the shelter!"

"All right!" Randi shouted. "Let's go!"

* * *

"Cool!" Randi murmured when she stepped inside the Best Buddies Animal shelter. All she could see were wire cages—rows and rows of them.

The cages were full of dogs and puppies, cats and kittens, rabbits, birds, and guinea pigs. There was even a cage with a green-and-brown curled-up snake. It made Randi shiver.

A woman wearing a long white shirt and black tights stepped out from behind the cages. "Welcome to Best Buddies," she said, smiling. "My name is Karen. If you'd like to pet some of the animals, I'll open the cages for you."

Randi walked over to a huge pen in the corner of the room. She peered inside.

The pen was full of little fluffy kittens! Ten of them!

"Would you like to go in?" Karen asked.

Randi smiled a huge smile. "I sure would!" she answered.

Karen opened the pen. Carefully Randi walked in. She took off her backpack and knelt down to play with the kittens.

The frisky little cats scampered all over her legs and tumbled about in front of her. They even climbed on her backpack! Randi played with them all.

Then she spotted a black-and-gray-striped kitten with white paws. It sat all by itself in one corner. Randi thought it looked lonely. "Can I hold that one?" she asked Karen.

"Sure," Karen answered. Randi picked up the kitten.

"We call him Socks," Karen said. "We hope to find a home for him soon."

Randi pressed her face into Socks's soft, warm fur. The kitten purred. "You're so cute," Randi whispered. "I would love to take you home with me."

The kitten snuggled up under Randi's chin. His fur tickled and made her giggle. She gently set him down.

A small red rubber ball lay in the pen. Randi rolled it toward Socks. He eyed it warily. Randi rolled it a little closer. Socks pounced on it. The toy made a loud *squeak!* The kitten leaped back, surprised.

Randi laughed. She rolled the ball toward the kitten again.

"Okay, Figure Eights! Time to head out," Carol announced.

Already? Randi thought. *Wow! I guess I spent the whole time playing with the kittens!*

"Sorry I can't take you home with me," she whispered to Socks. "Good-bye." She took one last look at all the animals in the shelter before she left.

"Okay—let's go, Figure Eights." Carol guided everyone to the door.

"Wait!" Randi shouted. "My backpack! I left my backpack inside the kitten pen!"

"Okay. We'll meet you at the car, Randi," Carol said.

A minute later Randi slid into Carol's backseat beside Anna and Kate.

When Carol pulled up in front of the ice rink, everyone thanked her for taking them on the trip. Then Randi raced after Anna into Mr. Mullen's pro shop.

"My dad can drive you home as soon as he closes the shop," Anna offered.

"Okay," Randi said. "I guess I'll do some homework till then."

She sat down on the floor next to a stack of skate boxes. She reached into her backpack for her math book. But instead of feeling something smooth and cold, she felt something soft. And fuzzy.

And breathing!

Randi opened her bag wide. There, inside, sat a black-and-gray-striped kitten—*Socks!*

5

The Plan

"Randi!" Anna gasped. "What are you doing with that kitten?"

"I—I don't know how he got in there," Randi stammered.

Anna folded her arms. "Oh, *sure*, Randi."

"It's true!" Randi protested. "I left my backpack in his pen. He must have crawled inside it!"

"Well—what are you going to do now?" Anna asked.

"I wish I could keep him." Randi sighed.

Anna shook her head. "You can't! Your parents said you weren't allowed to have a pet!"

Randi frowned. "I know. I guess I'll have to take him back."

Just then Socks blinked. He stretched his paws way out in front of him. He opened his mouth in a big kitten yawn.

"Oh! He's so *cute*, Randi!" Anna said. "I'd never be able to take him back."

Randi thought hard. "Maybe I don't have to," she said.

"What do you mean?" Anna asked.

"I have an idea." Randi smiled. "A great idea!"

Randi jumped up and ran to the phone. She dialed Information and asked for the phone number of Best Buddies Animal Shelter. Quickly she dialed the number.

"Hello—is this Karen?" Randi asked the woman who answered the phone. "This is Randi Wong. I just visited your shelter with the Figure Eights skating club."

"Hi, Randi," Karen said. "Can I help you with something?"

"I thought you might be looking for Socks the

kitten," Randi told her. "I have him here. He must have climbed into my bag accidentally."

"Oh! We were so worried about him!" Karen cried. "We were afraid he had gotten out of his pen. Don't worry, Randi. We'll come and pick him up right now."

"No!" Randi said quickly. "You don't have to pick him up. I want to adopt him!"

"Great!" Karen said. "Socks needs a good home! Your parents should come down to fill out the adoption papers and—"

"Well . . . my parents won't be able to come to the shelter until—uh—sometime next week," Randi interrupted.

There was a long pause.

"Can I keep Socks with me until then?" Randi asked. "Please?"

Randi crossed her fingers. She hoped Karen would agree to let her keep Socks.

"Well—I guess that's fine," Karen finally said. "But I'll expect your parents to come in by the end of the week. Okay?"

"No problem!" Randi said. "Thanks, Karen!" She hung up the phone.

"Randi!" Anna gasped. "What are you doing? You can't keep this kitten! Your parents think you're too young to have a pet!"

"Maybe I can convince them I'm *not* too young," Randi told Anna.

"I'll keep Socks all this week—and take good care of him—without telling Mom and Dad! That will prove I can handle a pet, even if I am busy with skating and homework and chores. Then Mom and Dad will let me keep Socks for sure. Won't they?"

6

The Incredible Disappearing Liver

"Hi, honey. How was your visit to the shelter?" Mrs. Wong asked when Randi walked into the house that evening.

"Great!" Randi replied. She held her backpack carefully in her arms so that she wouldn't squash Socks.

"I know you want to go get sponsors for the skate-a-thon," Mrs. Wong said. "I can take you out right now. Before dinner."

Not now! Randi thought. *I have to get Socks all settled in his new home first!*

"I—I want to go," Randi stammered. "But I have to finish my Sally Smith, Super Detective book first—for my book report."

"Okay," Mrs. Wong replied. "If that's what you want."

Randi sprinted upstairs to the bedroom she shared with Laurie. She closed the door and opened her backpack. She lifted out her brand-new kitten.

"Now, the first thing you need is a bed," she said. "And I know just what to make it from." She dashed into Henry's room, took his new skateboard box, and hurried back to her room.

Then she grabbed a small pillow from her bed and two of Laurie's doll blankets. She stuffed them inside the box.

"There," she said, placing Socks in his new bed. "Do you like it?"

The kitten pressed the pillow up and down with his front paws. Then he curled up and fell sound asleep.

He'll need a litter box also, thought Randi. She ran downstairs and grabbed some old newspapers. She shredded them into an empty shoe box. *That ought to do for now.*

And he should have something to play with,

Randi thought. She gave Socks some of Kristi's old hair ribbons and one of the twins' race cars. She set them next to him in his bed.

"Randi! Dinner!" her mother called from downstairs.

"Be right down," Randi yelled back.

She picked up the boxes and put them in the back of her closet. "Got to go, Socks. I'll leave the door open a crack so you have light and air."

She jogged down the stairs and into the dining room.

"Did you see lots of cute animals at the shelter, Baby Randi?" Henry asked.

Randi shot Henry a mean look. Then she told her family about the shelter. "I met a little kitten named Socks," she said. "He crawled right up against my neck. He loved me, and I loved him."

Mrs. Wong reached across the table and squeezed Randi's hand. "We're sorry you can't have a kitten right now, Randi. But a pet really is too much for you to take care of by yourself."

Randi gulped. She had to persuade her parents to let her have a pet. *And I might as well start right now,* she decided.

"Every family needs a pet," she began. "I think we should have a . . . a kitten. A gray-and-black-striped, furry one."

"We should?" her father asked. "Why?"

Randi thought hard. "Because kittens keep you company when you're home sick from school. And they scare away mice."

"That's true, Randi, but—" Mr. Wong started.

"Kittens eat table scraps too. And . . . and you can earn lots of money with a kitten," Randi interrupted.

"What? You can't earn money with a kitten!" Henry laughed.

"Yes, you can!" Randi snapped. "Some kittens model for cat food ads on TV. And they make tons of money."

Now Mr. Wong laughed too. "I'm sorry, Randi. Even if they do make tons of money, we're sticking to what we said. No pets."

Randi sighed. She'd have to figure out another way to convince her parents she needed a kitten.

"Hey! How many sponsors do you have for the skate-a-thon?" Kristi asked.

"Just three so far," Randi replied. She turned

to her mother. "Will you take me to the neighbors' after dinner to get some more pledges?"

Mrs. Wong nodded. "As long as it's right after dinner. Later on I have to give the twins and Laurie their baths."

"Right after dinner is great!" Randi smiled. *I'll gobble my food down,* she thought, *so I can check on Socks before we go.*

Then Randi saw what was for dinner.

Ugh! Liver! Her all-time nightmare meal!

"Yuck!" Henry clutched his throat. "I can't eat this!"

"Me neither." Kristi jabbed the liver with her fork.

"I baked a double chocolate chip layer cake for dessert," Mrs. Wong announced. She smiled. "No liver, no cake."

Henry and Kristi groaned. But Randi had an idea. A way to take care of her kitten *and* get sponsors all at once. She kicked Henry under the table. "Want to make a deal?" she whispered.

Henry glared at her, puzzled.

"I'll eat your liver if you sponsor me for the skate-a-thon," Randi explained.

"You got it!" Henry whispered back.

Randi nudged Kristi. "Will you sponsor me if I eat your liver?" she mumbled behind her hand.

Kristi grinned and gave Randi a thumbs-up.

"Henry," Randi whispered. "Get Mom and Dad's attention—"

Before she could finish her sentence, Henry started to cough—*loudly*. He pounded his chest and stuck out his tongue.

"Drink this, Henry." Mrs. Wong held out a glass of water.

"Can't," Henry choked. "I . . . need . . . air." He leaped off his chair and staggered into the kitchen. On the way, Randi saw him give her a little smile. She covered her mouth to hold in a giggle.

Mr. and Mrs. Wong jumped up and followed Henry into the kitchen. Moving fast, Randi spread her napkin next to Henry's plate. She slipped most of his liver into her napkin.

By the time Henry returned to the table, Kristi and Randi only had a couple of pieces of liver left on their plates too.

"Well, I see everybody ate their liver," Mrs. Wong said when dinner was over. "You all deserve a big piece of chocolate cake."

"May I have mine later?" Randi asked. "And may I be excused?"

"Sure, honey," her mom said. "I'll save some cake for you."

With her napkin in her pocket, Randi left the dining room. She sprinted up the stairs and into her bedroom.

Randi set the liver on the floor just outside her closet. She opened the closet door and peeked inside.

There was her kitten's box, right where she'd left it.

But there was no kitten inside!

"Socks!" Randi called. She turned everything in her closet upside down and inside out. "Where are you?" Her heart began to race.

Calm down, she told herself.

She searched her room.

Still no Socks.

"Oh! Where could he be?" she said aloud.

"Randi!" Mrs. Wong called from downstairs. "I'll be ready to get sponsors with you in five minutes!"

Yikes! Randi thought. *I have to find Socks! Quick!*

7

Lost and Found

Randi's heart pounded as she sprinted down the hall into Henry's room. "Are you in here, Socks?" she whispered.

But she couldn't find him anywhere. He wasn't in Jill's room. Or Kristi's room. Or the twins' room either.

I'd better check downstairs, Randi thought.

She raced into the kitchen, where Kristi and Henry were helping their mother with the dishes.

"Ready to go out for sponsors now, Randi?" Mrs. Wong asked.

"Yes," Randi answered. "I mean—no." *I want to get sponsors,* she thought. *But I can't go now. Not with Socks missing.*

"I'll be ready in a little while, okay?" she finally said.

"Don't make it too late," her mother warned. "Remember, I have to give the twins their baths."

"I won't," Randi said. She sprinted into the living room. There she found Mr. Wong playing with Michael and Mark. But she still hadn't found Socks.

Where is he? Randi wondered anxiously. *I looked everywhere!* She paused.

Almost everywhere, she realized. She raced up the stairs and into her parents' bedroom. She stepped inside and heard a sound—a tiny, squeaky meow. She looked up.

There, perched high on the curtain rod, was Socks!

"Get down!" Randi ordered. "Before Mom and Dad find you!"

Socks meowed, but he didn't move.

Randi raced back to her bedroom and returned with her brown, soggy napkin. "Yum! Liver!" She held the liver out to Socks.

Socks's nose twitched. His tail flicked. He me-

owed a long, loud meow and jumped onto Randi's parents' bed!

Randi scooped him up and dashed to her bedroom.

"Whew! That was scary," she said. She stroked the kitten while he gobbled his liver. "Never run away again, Socks."

She waited while the kitten finished eating and licked his paws.

"Now back to bed," Randi said, setting him in his bed in the closet. "I have to get sponsors. I can't let the Hot Shots down!" She slipped on her jacket and hurried out of her room.

"Mom! Where are you?" she called.

As she stood in the hall, she heard squeals of laughter coming from the bathroom. She looked inside. Her twin brothers were in the bath, neck deep in bubbles.

"I'm ready to go now, Mom," Randi announced.

Mrs. Wong looked up. "It's too late, honey. Your father and I are getting the twins and Laurie ready for bed."

Randi's heart sank. "But can't we go out for just a little while?" she begged.

Mrs. Wong shook her head. "Sorry, Randi, but it's almost your bedtime too. We'll come give you a kiss in a few minutes."

Randi heaved a heavy sigh. The skate-a-thon was only five days away! She needed twenty-five sponsors—soon!

Tomorrow I'll get a whole bunch! I really will! she promised herself.

She trudged back to her bedroom. She changed into her pajamas and crawled into bed.

Mr. Wong carried Laurie in and tucked her into bed.

As he crossed the room to give Randi a kiss, Mrs. Wong walked in. In her arms she carried a huge, messy ball of yarn. All different colors were tangled together.

"Whoa!" Mr. Wong said, staring at the yarn. "What happened there?"

"I'm not sure," Mrs. Wong replied. "I was going to do some knitting later tonight. Then I found my yarn like this! It will probably take me all night to untangle it!" She looked at Randi.

"You weren't playing with it, were you?" she asked.

"No, Mom," Randi answered.

"I didn't think so," Mrs. Wong said. "It must have been one of the twins or Laurie."

Randi glanced over at her closet, where Socks lay sleeping. *Could someone else have gotten into it?* she wondered.

"Well, give me my kiss good-night," Mrs. Wong said. She kissed Randi on the cheek.

Randi's parents turned to leave the room.

"Meow."

Randi froze. Her heart skipped a beat.

"Did you hear that?" Mr. Wong asked.

"What?" Randi's mom answered.

"That sound. It sounded—like a cat!" Mr. Wong said.

Mrs. Wong laughed. "How silly. There's no cat in here!"

"It was my stomach!" Randi burst out. "I guess it doesn't like the liver." She clutched her stomach.

Please don't meow again, Socks, she thought.

Mrs. Wong smiled and gently pulled Randi's

dad into the hallway. "Good night, Randi," she called.

"Good night, Mom. Good night, Dad." Randi scrunched down in her bed and pulled the comforter over her head. *Be quiet, Socks,* she begged. *And please be good so I can get some sponsors tomorrow!*

8

Caught!

On Tuesday afternoon Randi and all the Figure Eights met at the Seneca Hills Ice Arena for practice. Carol had everyone separate into teams and skate laps around the rink.

"I don't think I can do this much longer!" Kate moaned on the Hot Shots' sixth lap. "My legs are killing me!"

"Come on, guys!" Randi cheered. "You can do it!"

With Randi's help, the Hot Shots completed one last lap around the rink.

"Okay, team! Let's huddle!" Randi called. The Hot Shots formed a tight circle.

"We're getting really good," Randi told her

team. "If we keep working really hard, we're sure to beat the Speed Demons!"

"But they're still skating better than us," Kate pointed out.

The Hot Shots stole a glance at the Speed Demons as they circled the rink. The Speed Demons didn't look as if they were getting tired at all. The Hot Shots went back into a huddle.

"Kate's right," Max said. "And if the Speed Demons are skating better than us, that means they'll finish more laps than us at the skate-a-thon. If we want to win, we *have* to get more sponsors than they do."

"Did I hear someone say *sponsors*?" asked Woody's voice.

Randi whirled around and saw Woody standing behind her. "Hey! No spying!" Randi joked, punching him lightly in the arm.

"I wasn't spying," Woody protested. "I was just wondering how many sponsors you have."

Randi felt her face turn red. "None of your business!" she said. There was no way she could tell anyone the truth—that she still didn't have twenty-five sponsors.

46

"Ha! That's because you don't have *any* sponsors, do you?" Woody teased.

"Randi has twenty-five sponsors. Right, Randi?" Max said.

Randi felt awful, but what could she say? Her teammates would be so mad if they knew she only had five sponsors. Especially since the skate-a-thon was just four days away!

"Show Woody your sponsor list, Randi," Anna said. "Show him what a great captain you are!"

Randi swallowed hard. "Uh, I don't have my list with me," she said quickly. "Sorry, guys."

Woody turned toward his team. "Come on, Speed Demons! Let's keep practicing! We have to work hard if we're going to beat those Hot Shots!"

"Yeah!" the Speed Demons cried. "Beat the Hot Shots!"

Randi watched as Woody, Josh, Frederika, and Samantha took the ice again.

"Bring your sponsor list to our special practice tomorrow, Randi," Max said. "That will show Woody which team is going to win!"

47

"Yeah." Randi smiled weakly. Then she added to herself, "That's what I'm afraid of."

Randi walked up to her house later that afternoon.

I have to find a way to get at least some *sponsors today—or the Hot Shots are going to be really mad at me!* she thought.

She pushed open her front door.

"I've told you a dozen times not to try on my hair scrunchies!" Kristi yelled as Randi walked inside.

Randi frowned. "I didn't touch your scrunchies."

"Then who scattered them all over my bedroom?" Kristi asked.

Randi thought for a minute. "Maybe Henry did it. Just to be a pain in the neck."

Kristi paused. "That's it!" she said. "Henry did it!" She turned and marched toward the kitchen. "Henry!" she shouted.

Randi ran up the stairs to say hello to Socks. She threw open her closet door. Socks looked up at Randi and gave a soft meow.

"There's my kitty!" Randi cooed. "Did you miss me while I was gone?" She picked Socks up and cradled him in her arms. Then, out of the corner of her eye, she saw something in Socks's bed. Something yellow.

"Hey! What's this?" Randi bent down and picked up the yellow object. She gasped.

It was Kristi's best scrunchie!

Randi bit her lip. She held Socks out in front of her and studied him. *Oh, no!* she thought. *Socks is the one who messed up Kristi's scrunchies!*

"Socks," Randi scolded. "You have to stay in your box when I'm not home. I can't let anyone know about you yet!"

Guess I'll have to keep a close watch on him, Randi thought, petting him. *At least for today.*

She heard the front door open. "I'm home!" Mrs. Wong called out.

Rats! I wanted to ask Mom to take me for sponsors, Randi thought. *But I can't go now! I have to stay with Socks.*

Randi put the kitten in his bed and left the closet door open just a crack.

She stared at the closet. Socks didn't set even one paw out of it.

Maybe I can leave you for a little while, Randi thought—until she saw the closet door slowly swinging open.

Socks stepped out, glanced at her, then ran from the room.

Randi raced down the hall after him.

Socks turned left into Kristi's room. *Oh, no!* Randi thought. *Don't go in there!*

Randi charged into Kristi's room just in time to see Socks jump into the basket where Kristi kept her scrunchies. One by one, he batted each scrunchie out of the basket with his paw.

Randi scooped Socks up. She shoved Kristi's scrunchies back into their basket. Then she raced back to her room and put Socks in his box.

"Randi!" Mrs. Wong called from downstairs. "Can you come down here, please?"

Randi left her room, shutting the door tight behind her. *At least that way, Socks won't be able to cause too much trouble,* she thought. *And maybe I can leave the house to get some more sponsors!*

She raced down the stairs. "Hi, Mom!" she said.

"Hi, honey," Mrs. Wong said. "Can you help me start dinner?"

Randi followed Mrs. Wong into the kitchen. "Mom, could you take me to get some sponsors tonight?"

Mrs. Wong removed a stack of plates from the kitchen cabinet. "Sorry. I have my aerobics class on Tuesday nights. Remember?" she answered.

Randi sat down in a heap at the kitchen table. *How am I ever going to get sponsors?* she wondered.

Then she remembered—her sponsor list! She had promised she'd bring it to practice tomorrow to show everyone she had twenty-five sponsors!

"Oh, no!" she moaned. "What am I going to do?"

9

Sally Smith, Super Sponsor

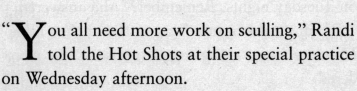

"You all need more work on sculling," Randi told the Hot Shots at their special practice on Wednesday afternoon.

With Randi leading them, the Hot Shots circled the rink. As Randi tried to focus on sculling, she thought about her almost empty sponsor sheet. What would she tell her teammates when they asked to see it?

She glanced back at the Hot Shots. They weren't putting enough effort into their sculling. And if they didn't get serious about their skating, there was no way they were ever going to win the skate-a-thon. Not when Woody's team had so many sponsors—and Randi had just five!

"Let's move faster!" Randi yelled. "Come on, Hot Shots! Give it your all!"

They had only gone partway around the rink when Anna skated to a stop. "Randi! We've been skating . . . for hours. I think it's time . . . to quit," she huffed, out of breath.

"Yeah," Kate agreed. "I think we've practiced enough."

"Well—okay," Randi said, disappointed.

The Hot Shots skated over to the side of the rink together.

"Hey!" Max said. "Time to check on sponsors!" He turned to Randi. "Did you remember to bring your sheet?"

Randi gulped. "Uh—sure. But I don't have it with me. It's in the locker room—in my bag."

"Well, go get it!" Max said.

Randi's stomach felt as if it were tied in little knots. What was she going to do? She couldn't show the Hot Shots her list. Not with only five sponsors on it!

Then, suddenly, it came to her. A plan! She had to move fast if it was going to work. And she wasn't sure she could pull it off. But it was her only chance to show everyone that she had twenty-five sponsors—just as she had said.

"No problem," she told her teammates. "I'll get it right now!"

She shot out of the rink and into the locker room.

She pulled her backpack out of her locker and fished around inside for her sponsor sheet. She took out a pen.

On the list, right underneath Henry's name, Randi wrote, "JENNY BROWN." "That sounds nice," she said. "And I love the name Cindy." Under "JENNY BROWN," she wrote "CINDY STONE."

"Jill's friends in Silver Blades all have cool names too." Randi wrote, "NIKKI SIMON, TORI CARSEN, DANIELLE PANATI, ALEX BEEKMAN," and the names of the rest of the Silver Blades she knew.

Randi counted all the names on her list, including her real sponsors—her mom, her dad, Jill, Kristi, and Henry. "Only twenty!" she groaned. "Who else can I add?" She paused. Nothing came to her.

"Come on, think!" Randi ordered herself.

She snapped her fingers. "I know! I'll use the characters from Sally Smith, Super Detective!"

Quickly she scribbled down "SALLY SMITH" and the name of Sally's best friend, "ROSIE PEPPER." Then she added "PETER WRINKLE," "JOE FLASH," and "SUZIE SHIVER."

Randi counted the names again. "Yes! Twenty-five!"

She grabbed her backpack and ran through the doors to the lobby. Anna, Max, and Kate were already walking toward her. "Hey, Captain Randi!" Kate said. "Let's see your extra-long sponsor sheet!"

"Yeah!" Max said. "Show me the sponsors!"

"Here they are!" Randi said, holding out her list. "See? Twenty-five sponsors." She started to shove the list back into her bag.

"I wonder if we asked any of the same people," Anna said. She snatched Randi's list from her hand.

"I doubt it!" Randi told her. She reached for the paper, but Anna snapped it away.

Please don't read past Henry's name, Randi begged silently. *Please.*

"Hmmm," Anna said, running her finger down the list. "Nikki Simon. Tori Carsen. Danielle Panati. Hey! You got *all* the Silver Blades to sponsor you!"

"Yeah," Randi muttered, faking a smile. "Cool, huh?"

She felt her ears getting hot and her hands getting cold and sweaty. "Don't read any more," she said, trying to sound calm. "It's really boring." She grabbed at the paper.

But Anna held on tight.

Randi felt sick. She knew what was coming next.

Anna continued to read. "Rosie Pepper? Peter Wrinkle? And *Sally Smith*! These aren't real people! They're characters in the Sally Smith, Super Detective books! I can't believe it! You lied to us, Randi!"

10

More Trouble

"How could you do that?" Max demanded. He narrowed his eyes. "How could you make up names to put on your list?"

"Yeah," Anna chimed in. She stuck her nose close to Randi's. "We're your teammates. How could you lie to us?"

Randi's face turned bright red. She could hardly look at her friends. "They're not *all* made up," she answered in a small voice. "Mom, Dad, Jill, Kristi, and Henry really sponsored me."

Anna parked her hand on her hip. "That's it? You only have *five* real sponsors?" Her voice grew louder and louder.

Kate shook her head in disbelief. "You're our

captain, Randi. You should have more sponsors than anyone!"

"But there's a good reason—" Randi started to explain.

"It better be *real* good," Max grumbled.

Randi took a deep breath. "It's because of my kitten."

"You have a kitten?" Max and Kate asked at the same time.

Randi sighed. "Yeah. I'm trying to keep him a secret from my parents. But it's really hard. He keeps wandering around and getting into trouble. First I found him hanging on my parents' curtains. Then he messed up all Kristi's scrunchies. So I have to watch him a lot. And when I'm not watching him, there's homework to do, or my chores. Then I have no time to get sponsors."

"I know you're taking care of a kitten," Kate said. "But—"

"But what about the Hot Shots?" Anna interrupted. "We're a team, Randi. And you're our captain. You're supposed to *lead* us."

"Wait, guys!" Randi pleaded. "Give me another chance! I *can* be a good captain! You'll see.

I'm going to get all twenty-five sponsors. Real ones. And I'm going to start getting them today—right after practice."

"You only have tonight, Thursday, and Friday left, Randi—three days until the skate-a-thon," Max reminded her.

Randi nodded. "I know. Believe me—I know!"

Randi rushed straight home from the rink that afternoon. *I'll get Mom and go out for sponsors right away,* she thought.

When Randi banged through the front door, she found her mom putting her coat on.

"Let's go, Mom," Randi said. "We need to move fast." She took her mother's hand and pulled her toward the door.

"Hold on, Randi," Mrs. Wong laughed. "I need to get everyone together before we leave."

"You mean *everybody's* going with us to get sponsors? Henry and Kristi and the twins and everybody?" Randi asked, confused.

"No, honey," Mrs. Wong said. "Don't you remember what day this is?"

Randi thought a minute. "Wednesday?"

Her mother nodded. "Yes, it's Wednesday. But it's also Kristi's birthday. Pizza and a movie tonight—remember?"

Oh, no! Randi thought. *I forgot all about Kristi's party. By the time we get home, it will be too late to go out for sponsors!*

Randi frowned. *Now I have only two days to get twenty sponsors!*

11

Terror on the Ice!

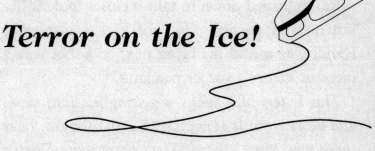

When Randi woke up the next morning, she heard Henry's angry voice coming from downstairs.

What's he yelling about? Randi wondered.

She crawled out of bed and crept over to the stairs. She hung over the railing. That way, she could hear Henry's voice more clearly.

"It was my *favorite* soccer pennant!" he yelled. "*Someone* ripped it to shreds!"

"Calm down, Henry," Mrs. Wong said. "Yelling won't do any good. I'm sure we'll figure out what happened to it."

Randi gulped. She walked over to her closet and peered inside. Socks lay in his bed, sleeping peacefully. *Whew!* Randi thought. *What a relief.*

Randi leaned down to take a closer look at her kitten—and gasped. *Oh, no!* It was just what Randi was afraid of. Lying next to Socks was a piece of Henry's soccer pennant!

This is terrible! Socks is getting me into more and more trouble every day, Randi thought. *First there was Mom's yarn. Then there were Kristi's scrunchies. And now Henry's pennant is totally destroyed!*

"What am I going to do with you, Socks?" Randi wondered aloud. She looked down at her kitten, sleeping so peacefully. "Please try to be good!" she pleaded. "Or I'll have to give you back!"

Randi went downstairs and ate her breakfast in a flash. She didn't want Henry or her mom asking her about Henry's pennant.

Then she hurried upstairs to get changed. There was no school because of a teachers' conference, but she had called a special skate-a-thon practice at the rink.

She peeked in at Socks, who was still sleeping in his little bed. He looked so cute!

But could Randi trust him alone in the house while she went to practice? The answer was a big fat no. What was she going to do?

"Over here," Anna called to Randi when she walked into the locker room. "Did you have any luck getting sponsors yesterday? You only have two days left, remember."

Randi cringed. She couldn't tell Anna she hadn't collected any sponsors last night. So she didn't answer.

Instead, she sat down on a bench and opened her backpack. "Look, Anna," she whispered. A black, stripy, furry head poked out of the pack.

"You brought Socks to the *rink*?" Anna asked. "Are you crazy? What are you going to do with him during practice?"

Randi smiled. "He can sleep in my backpack. That's what he's been doing all morning anyway."

Anna glanced around at the other skaters in

the locker room. "I hope no adults see him," she warned. "They wouldn't like the idea of a kitten in here."

"Don't worry," Randi said. "He'll stay in this bag until—"

Suddenly Socks sprang out of the backpack. Randi tried to grab for him, but she didn't grab fast enough.

The frisky ball of fluff leaped from the bench to the floor. Then he shot through the locker room door!

"We have to catch him, Anna!" Randi cried. She took off after the tiny kitten, with Anna close behind. Socks streaked down the hallway and across the lobby.

Surprised skaters stopped and watched the two girls flying after the tiny kitten.

"Grab him, quick!" Anna yelled.

But Socks was too fast. He shot through another doorway.

Oh, no! Randi thought. *He's headed for the rink!* She darted after him—and saw him streak onto the glassy ice, where the Hot Shots and the Speed Demons were warming up!

"Whoa!" "Look out!" they yelled. They swerved out of the way as the runaway kitten slid past them.

Socks dug his claws into the ice to stop himself, but it was too slippery.

The terrified kitten whooshed straight across the ice on his tummy. He stopped inches before slamming into the far wall.

"Stay there, Socks!" Randi yelled, sliding across the ice in her sneakers. She scooped up the kitten. He clung to her shirt and nestled under her chin. Randi felt his heart beating wildly.

"Oh, Anna," Randi said as she stepped off the ice. "No matter what I try, I can't keep Socks under control. And as long as I can't keep him under control, I can't get any sponsors! What am I going to do?"

12

Mystery Fish

Randi tried hard not to worry about Socks—
or wonder what he was doing—while she
was collecting pledges with her mom on Friday
night.

What else could I do? Randi thought. *The
skate-a-thon is tomorrow. I had to leave Socks
home alone so I could collect pledges. Otherwise,
I would* never *get the twenty-five sponsors I
promised the Hot Shots.*

Randi rang the front doorbell of the next house
on the block. *He'll be good,* she thought. *He just
has to be.* She glanced behind her to be sure that
her mom was watching from the car.

Mrs. Wong gave her a little wave. Randi waved back.

Randi pressed the doorbell again. Inside, a dog barked. *Please,* she begged. *Please let them sponsor me.*

A woman opened the door.

Randi smiled her biggest smile. "Hello," she said. "I belong to the Figure Eights skating club. We're having a skate-a-thon to raise money for all the animals at the Best Buddies Animal Shelter. I was wondering if—"

"If I would sponsor you?" the woman broke in. She smiled. "I think you're skating for a very good cause."

Randi sighed with relief. All right! Another sponsor!

"But I'm afraid you're the third skater to ask me," the woman continued. "I'm sorry, but I can't sponsor anyone else."

"Oh," Randi said in a tiny voice. "Thank you anyway." Fighting back tears, she dashed to her parents' minivan.

"Any luck?" Mrs. Wong asked.

"No!" Randi cried. "What am I going to do? I

only got five pledges tonight! That means I only have ten sponsors!"

"Ten is pretty good, honey," her mother said.

"It's horrible!" Randi wailed. "I'm the captain of the team! I said I'd get more sponsors than anybody! Now the skate-a-thon is tomorrow. And everybody has more sponsors than me!"

Slowly Mrs. Wong drove the van away from the curb. "Maybe being the team captain was too much for you," she said softly. "Especially on top of homework, and skate practice, and your chores around the house . . ."

Not to mention a wild kitten, Randi thought.

Mrs. Wong turned onto their street. "Ten sponsors will have to be good enough," she said. "We're going home now."

"Wait!" Randi shouted. "Can't we stop at just a few more—"

"Sorry, Randi," Mrs. Wong said. "It's way past your bedtime. You'll need a good night's sleep to skate your best tomorrow."

Randi felt awful. Tonight had been her last chance to get sponsors. And she'd blown it.

That means one thing, she admitted to herself

sadly as she walked into her house. *The Hot Shots can't win. And I'm the most horrible captain in the world.*

Randi hung her head. Things couldn't get any worse.

She went into the living room and found Mr. Wong watching a movie with Henry, the twins, and Laurie.

"Hi, Randi!" Mr. Wong said. He pressed the Pause button on the VCR. "How did it go? Did you get lots of sponsors?"

Randi plunked down on the sofa beside him. "No. I didn't get *nearly* enough," she moaned.

"I'm sorry, honey," he said.

"Eeek!" A shriek burst from Kristi's room.

Randi and her father ran to the stairs. Kristi stood at the top. "One of my goldfish is missing!" she wailed. "I had six, and now there are only five!"

"That's impossible," Mr. Wong said. "Are you sure you counted right?"

"I think so," Kristi answered.

Randi felt a huge lump form in her throat. How could one of Kristi's goldfish be *missing*?

There was only one answer she could think of. And she hoped it was the *wrong* answer.

She ran to her room. *Oh, Socks! Please don't let it be your fault!* she thought.

Randi found Socks in his place in her closet. She lifted him up. *Oh, no!* His face and paws were *wet!*

"Socks! How could you?" Randi scolded the kitten. "How could you eat Kristi's goldfish?"

Then Randi stopped. *It's not his fault,* she realized. *It's my fault.* I'm *the one who didn't have enough time to take care of him.* I'm *the one who left him at home with the goldfish!*

Randi hugged Socks. Tears streamed down her face.

Now I've ruined everything! The Hot Shots will never win the skate-a-thon. And I'll have to tell Mom and Dad about what happened to Kristi's fish. They'll never let me keep Socks! I'll have to give him up.

"Oh, Socks," Randi cried into the kitten's fur. "This is the absolute worst night of my entire life!"

13

The Big Day

Randi woke up early the next morning. It was Saturday. The day of the skate-a-thon.

But she didn't feel like getting up. She felt like hiding under the covers.

Today is the day I tell Mom and Dad about Socks, she remembered. *Today is the day the Hot Shots lose the skate-a-thon. Today is the worst day in the world.*

She dragged herself out of bed. She checked to see that Socks was asleep in his box. Then she went downstairs to breakfast.

She paused outside the kitchen doorway. She heard her mom talking to Kristi.

"Don't worry, honey," Mrs. Wong said. "I'll

ask Henry if he knows what happened to the fish. Or maybe one of the twins got into the tank. Either way, we'll figure out what happened."

Randi winced. Kristi would be furious when she found out what had *really* happened to the fish. Randi decided to wait until after the skate-a-thon to tell her.

Randi walked into the kitchen.

"Good morning, dear," Mrs. Wong said.

I wish *it was a good morning,* Randi thought.

She glanced down and saw Laurie playing on the kitchen floor. Laurie giggled at one of her toys—a wind-up, roller-skating bear. It played a bass drum as it skated around and around. It reminded Randi of skating laps around the ice rink.

Randi giggled too. "This toy is really cute!" she said. She picked it up and set it on the kitchen table. It skated around the table, nearly knocking over Kristi's cereal bowl.

"Watch it!" Kristi called, catching her breakfast before it spilled.

This thing could go around and around forever! Randi thought.

Hey! That's it! Randi paused. She stared at the

toy. *Now I know how the Hot Shots can still win the skate-a-thon!*

Randi felt a huge smile spread across her face. Suddenly she couldn't wait to get to the rink. She couldn't wait to prove to her teammates that she could lead them to victory, even if she didn't have twenty-five sponsors!

When Randi walked into the rink, she saw Anna, Max, and Kate warming up at one end. Woody and the Speed Demons were warming up at the other.

"So, did you get all twenty-five sponsors?" Max asked Randi as soon as he spotted her.

"Nope, I only got thirteen. But I—"

"I can't believe you, Randi!" Kate blurted out. "You promised!"

"Wait!" Randi cried. "I don't need to have twenty-five sponsors. I have a plan!"

"Oh, no! Not another one of your plans, Randi," Anna moaned.

"Wait—this is a really good one. I'm going to skate a ton of laps," Randi explained. "Way more than anybody else."

Kate looked confused. "So?"

"If our team skates more laps, it will make up for not having as many sponsors," Randi explained. "Our sponsors will give us money for all the extra laps we do—and we'll still win!"

"But the Speed Demons are good skaters, Randi. You said it yourself. They're going to be hard to beat!" Anna pointed out.

Randi patted her stomach. "I ate four waffles, three pieces of toast, and a huge bowl of Honey Flakes for breakfast. I'll be able to skate forever." She paused. "It will work. I promise!"

"Okay, Randi," Max said. "Your plan *better* work."

Randi smiled at her teammates. "I won't let you down."

A bell clanged, signaling the start of the skate-a-thon. Randi heard a huge cheer. There were tons of people watching from the bleachers.

Too bad Mom and Dad had a wedding to go to and couldn't come today, Randi thought. *This is totally cool!*

Everyone lined up at the start. Another bell

clanged. The Speed Demons and Hot Shots took off!

They started with forward crossovers, followed by backward crossovers. On the third lap they bunny-hopped. On the fourth they sculled forward. On the fifth they sculled backward. Then they started all over again.

Each time the skaters passed Carol, she held up a big sign with a number on it. It was the number of laps they had skated.

After nine laps, Randi noticed Samantha hobbling off the ice. Pretty soon Josh and Frederika limped off too. *They're quitting already,* Randi said to herself. *But not me!*

Three laps later, Kate stumbled up behind Randi. "I've . . . had . . . enough," she puffed. "I'm stopping."

Max wobbled over. "Me too. I'm pooped."

"That's okay," Randi called, speeding off. "I'll skate enough extra laps for both of you."

Later, when Randi passed Carol, the number on her sign had gotten up to fourteen.

Whew! Randi thought as she brushed hair off

her hot, sticky cheek. *I've never skated this long before.*

She winced. Pain shot through her pinched toes.

I can't quit, she told herself. *I have to keep my promise to skate longer than the Speed Demons.*

She glided past Anna. "How are you doing?" Randi called.

"I quit," Anna mumbled. "Fourteen laps are enough for me!"

Anna stumbled off the ice. *Who's left?* Randi wondered.

Woody skated up next to her. She noticed that his face was bright red. Sweat streaked his cheeks. "You . . . okay?" she asked, trying to catch her breath.

"I guess," Woody panted.

It's just the two of us, Randi realized. *I have to skate longer than Woody!*

On their second time around the rink together, Woody gave out a big sigh. "I'm beat!" he mumbled. "You're on your own, Randi." He staggered off the ice.

Now Randi was the only skater. Her legs felt like two limp noodles, and she was dying to follow Woody to the bleachers.

No! she realized. *I can't quit yet.*

Randi skated one more lap. Then she skated a second and a third. She felt as though the rink were growing bigger and bigger with every lap.

At the end of the fourth lap, she caught her toe pick and almost fell.

I have to go on, she told herself. *I have to do it for the Hot Shots.*

Teetering and tottering, she started around the rink for her twentieth lap.

And for this lap, she had to scull backward! The hardest lap of all!

She bent her knees, turned her toes in toward each other, and pushed her blades against the ice. But she barely moved. With the little bit of energy she had left, she pushed harder.

Slowly, slowly she moved backward. *I don't think I can make it all the way around the rink like this,* she thought, worried.

But just when she thought she couldn't scull

one more inch, she glanced up. Anna, Max, and Kate were waving their arms and cheering. "Hang in there, Randi! You can do it!" they called.

Suddenly the cheers grew louder. Woody and the Speed Demons were cheering too! And so was everyone else in the bleachers!

"Ran-di! Ran-di! Ran-di!"

Randi forgot her pinched toes and her worn-out legs.

She ignored her pounding heart and her panting breath.

She focused all her energy on getting around the rink.

Just one more push, she told herself.

She gave one last push and crossed the finish line. The Hot Shots crowded around her, cheering.

Randi smiled, exhausted. She had led her team to victory!

Moments later Carol's voice sounded over the loudspeaker. "I'm happy to announce the winning team."

The Hot Shots huddled together. They were sure they had won. And they couldn't wait to hear their names announced!

No one made a sound as Carol spoke. "The winning team is . . ." She paused. "The Speed Demons!"

Randi gasped. "But—But what about all those extra laps I skated?" she whispered.

"Come on! Let's go ask Carol about it right now!" Anna said.

"You guys were great," Carol told the Hot Shots. "But even though Randi skated all those extra laps, it wasn't enough. You needed more sponsors."

Randi's shoulders slumped. Tears welled up in her eyes. "I can't believe it. I tried so hard."

She turned to her teammates. "I'm really sorry, guys. I know I let you down. Are you all mad at me?"

"Yeah," Kate said softly. "I really wanted to win."

"Me too," Max agreed.

"Why the sad faces, guys?" Carol asked.

"Randi didn't get enough sponsors," Max said. "That's why we lost!"

"That isn't what's important," Carol pointed out. "Randi may not have gotten as many sponsors as the rest of you, but she sure did try her best out on the ice today. And that's what really counts—doing your best."

She walked over to Randi and gave her shoulder a little squeeze. "Good job today, Randi." Carol smiled. "I'll see you all at practice on Tuesday," she called. Then she turned and left the rink.

"Maybe Carol is right," Anna said softly. "Randi did try really hard."

"Yeah," Max agreed, starting to smile. "I have to admit, you were pretty cool out there on the ice all by yourself."

Kate put her arm around Randi. "We're still a *little* mad at you," she said. "But even if you messed up, you're still our friend, Randi!"

"I've made up my mind," Randi announced. "I'm telling Mom and Dad about Socks, and I'm taking him back to the shelter."

Randi sat next to Anna in Mr. Mullen's car.

"Too bad," Anna said. "I know how much you love him."

Just thinking about saying good-bye to her kitten made Randi feel sad. But she had to. He had caused too much trouble for her friends and family. Not to mention her family's fish!

Mr. Mullen dropped Randi off in front of her house. She raced inside and dropped her skate bag in the hall.

"I'm home," she yelled. "Where is everybody?"

"In the living room, Randi," her mother called. "Please come in here right now!"

Uh-oh. Mom sounds mad, Randi thought. *What's going on?*

The moment Randi stepped into the living room, she knew what was going on.

On the sofa sat her mother, the twins, Henry, and Kristi.

And curled up next to Mrs. Wong—was Socks!

14

Good-bye, Socks

Randi gulped. "Where . . . where did you find him?"

"In my room, staring at my fish tank," Kristi answered. "And the five fish I have left!"

Randi shuddered. Good thing he didn't eat another fish! she thought.

She walked over to the sofa and picked up the kitten. "I was going to tell you about Socks, Mom. I really was."

"Good," Mrs. Wong said. "Because I'd really like to know how this kitten got into our house."

Randi cleared her throat. She told her mother the whole story.

"So *Socks* tangled up my yarn," Mrs. Wong said, "and messed up Kristi's scrunchies—"

"And destroyed my favorite pennant," Henry burst out.

"And ate my goldfish!" Kristi cried.

Randi sighed. "I'm really sorry about your pennant and your fish. I'll buy you both new ones with my allowance. Promise."

Randi turned to her mother. "You and Dad were right. Taking care of a kitten is a big job. Way too big for me to handle."

Mrs. Wong stood up. "I'm glad you realize that what you did was wrong, Randi." She sighed. "I guess we'd better get that kitten back to the shelter right now."

"Okay. I'll wait in the car, Mom," Randi mumbled.

Randi slid into her parents' minivan. She clutched Socks close to her.

"I tried so hard to keep you," she whispered to the kitten. "I'm going to miss you so much!"

Mrs. Wong got into the car and fastened her seat belt.

Randi heard a car pull up behind them. She turned. "Hey! That's Anna and her father!" she said. "I wonder what they're doing here."

Anna raced over to Randi. "Guess what?" she cried. "You don't have to take Socks back to the shelter!"

Randi crinkled her nose. "What do you mean?"

"Dad said *I* could have him. We can go to the shelter to fill out the papers right now! We'll keep him in the pro shop. And you can play with him every time you come to the rink!"

"Anna, that's so great!" Randi exclaimed.

She hugged the kitten one more time before handing him to her best friend. "See you in your new home, Socks," she said.

Anna took the kitten. "Dad says Socks can be the pro shop mascot."

Randi laughed. "You mean the pro shop mas-cat!"

About the Author

Effin Older is the author of many children's books published in the United States and abroad.

Effin lived in New Zealand for fourteen years. She currently lives in a tiny village in Vermont with her husband, Jules, and her white husky, Sophie. She has twin daughters named Amber and Willow.

When Effin isn't writing children's books, she likes to take long walks with Sophie, ride her mountain bike, and cross-country ski.

If you glided right through

jump into the SILVER BLADES series, featuring
Randi Wong's big sister Jill and her friends.

Look for these titles at your bookstore or library: